STAR WARS™

GALAXY OF
ADVENTURES

Written by
Meredith Rusu

DISNEY

LUCASFILM
PRESS

Los Angeles • New York

Printed in the United States of America

First Edition, September 2019
1 3 5 7 9 10 8 6 4 2
FAC-029261-19221
Library of Congress Control Number on file
ISBN 978-1-368-04557-5

Visit the official *Star Wars* website at: www.starwars.com.

SUSTAINABLE
FORESTRY
INITIATIVE

Certified Sourcing

www.sfiprogram.org
SFI-01415

CONTENTS

A long time ago in a galaxy far,
far away. . . .

In the *Star Wars* galaxy,
every day can be an adventure!

Luke Skywalker, a humble farm boy living on the desert planet Tatooine, dreamed of becoming something more. That dream came true the day he joined the Rebellion: a courageous group of heroes fighting against the evil Empire that controlled the galaxy. Luke wanted to help the Rebellion in their quest to end the Empire's tyranny. And along the way, he discovered he was destined to become a Jedi Knight: a powerful warrior who could use the Force—the energy connecting and surrounding all living creatures—for good.

Together with his friends—rebel leader Princess Leia, rogue pilot Han Solo, Jedi Master Obi-Wan Kenobi, and more—Luke would confront the Empire's dark warrior, Darth Vader. But victory wouldn't be an easy task. From epic battles on distant planets to starship clashes in the depths of space, these heroes would overcome monumental odds to change the course of the universe and their own destinies.

A galaxy of adventures awaits!

THE FORCE

Invisible yet ever present, the mysterious Force is the energy a Jedi uses for good—or a Sith uses for evil.

The Force surrounds and flows through all living creatures. Some individuals are "Force-sensitive" and can use the Force to do incredible things, like jump super high or run super fast.

Young Force-sensitive children would be brought to the Jedi Academy to become Jedi Knights. Padawans (or Jedi in training) would have a Grand Jedi Master as their first teacher. "Clear your mind," the teacher would instruct, "and let the Force flow through you."

Of course, with the wrong teacher, the Force could also be used for great evil. Sith are the opposite of the Jedi. Violent and selfish, these warriors use anger and aggression to control the dark side of the Force. Doing so allows them great power, but it also causes great suffering.

Not everyone in the galaxy believes in the Force, but those who do realize its strength. A common expression among rebel leaders is "May the Force be with you." It's their way of saying "Good luck." And in their fight against the all-mighty Empire, the rebels need all the help they can get!

LIGHTSABERS

Part sword, part laser, and all-around powerful, these blades of light can be used by noble Jedi to defend freedom—or by evil Sith to destroy it.

With the push of a button, a lightsaber ignites and its glowing blade instantly appears. These weapons are so powerful, they can cut through almost anything— even the hull of a spaceship! Jedi use them in battle and to block laser blasts.

One thing a lightsaber can't cut through is another lightsaber. So when two opponents clash in a lightsaber duel, sparks literally fly!

Rare kyber crystals are what power lightsabers. The kyber crystal a Jedi chooses determines the blade's color. Lightsabers come in many styles and colors—like green, blue, purple, and black. Some even have double

blades! Sith Lords usually wield deadly red lightsabers. Luke Skywalker used a blue lightsaber until it was lost in battle with Darth Vader. Then he made a new one that glowed green.

It takes years of practice to master lightsaber technique. But in the hands of the right hero, this weapon can help save the galaxy.

YODA

Every Jedi Master knows that when it comes to the Force, size matters not. Yoda is a nine-hundred-year-old Grand Jedi Master, and though he stands just over half a meter tall, he's one of the strongest Force-wielding warriors in the galaxy.

Before the Empire came to power, Yoda led the peaceful Jedi Order with courage and wisdom. He carried a green lightsaber and became a blur of flips and acrobatics during battle. He once fought the evil Count Dooku on the planet Geonosis when Dooku threatened to kill Yoda's fellow Jedi Obi-Wan Kenobi and Anakin Skywalker. Though Yoda entered the battle walking with a cane, Count Dooku soon learned he was in for the duel of his life.

Yoda's accomplishments can be measured not just

by his own success but by the success of the many students he trained. Young Padawans often had him as their first instructor. Yoda even helped teach Luke Skywalker to become a Jedi Master.

At first, Yoda's fragile, elderly appearance didn't exactly inspire confidence for Luke. But Yoda showed him that strength comes from within when he lifted Luke's crashed X-wing ship from the murky swamp waters of the planet Dagobah—using nothing but the Force! "Done it can be," Yoda told Luke. "As long as believe in yourself, you do."

Yoda is the only Jedi Master who talks backward. No one is exactly sure why. But as Yoda would say, "Matter, it does not." Yoda's wisdom inspired generations of Jedi, teaching them that fear is the path to the dark side, and how to use the Force for knowledge and defense, never attack. Yoda's size might be small, but his impact on the course of the galaxy is immeasurable.

QUI-GON JINN

"Feel, don't think. Use your instincts." Those were the words of Qui-Gon Jinn, a brave yet sometimes unconventional Jedi Master.

Qui-Gon was trained by Jedi Master Dooku (before Dooku left the Jedi Order), and he later trained Obi-Wan Kenobi. Bold and decisive, Qui-Gon believed that living in the moment was the best way to use the Force. He often instructed Obi-Wan to concentrate on the here and now rather than letting worries cloud his judgment.

During a mission to save the planet Naboo's Queen Amidala from an attack by the Trade Federation, Qui-Gon made an emergency landing on the planet Tatooine. It was there he met Anakin Skywalker: a boy so strong in the Force, Qui-Gon became convinced the child was the Chosen One, a hero who would restore balance to the Force, according to Jedi prophecies.

Qui-Gon brought Anakin before the Jedi Council, but the elders insisted Anakin was too old to begin Jedi training. Yoda, especially, sensed fear in the boy—fear that could be used by the dark side.

In a move uncommon for a Jedi, Qui-Gon went against the Council's wishes and said he would train the boy himself. But before he could do so, he and Obi-Wan came face to face with a powerful enemy—the Sith Darth Maul. During the battle for freedom on the planet Naboo, Darth Maul cornered the two Jedi and killed Qui-Gon. Obi-Wan defeated Darth Maul just in time to reach Qui-Gon's side and hear his dying wish: that Anakin be trained in the ways of the Force.

Obi-Wan kept his promise to his master. And though reluctant, the Jedi Council agreed Anakin could be trained. Qui-Gon would never see the prophecy come to fruition, but it was his determination that set it in motion.

OBI-WAN KENOBI

Patient and wise, Obi-Wan was a member of the Jedi Order for many years and a hero of the Clone Wars. His own master, Qui-Gon Jinn, taught him to trust his instincts, saying "Focus determines your reality." Later, Obi-Wan took it upon himself to train the most powerful Jedi of all—a young Padawan named Anakin Skywalker. It was prophesied that Anakin was the Chosen One, who would bring balance to the Force.

But Obi-Wan didn't anticipate how difficult it would be to train a headstrong apprentice like Anakin. And as Anakin's confidence grew, he became aggressive and turned to the dark side of the Force. Obi-Wan did everything he could to prevent his Padawan from being lured away by evil. But they ultimately clashed in a duel on the volcanic planet Mustafar, and Anakin

became the dreaded Sith Lord Darth Vader. Crushed, Obi-Wan fought to save the Jedi Order, but with Darth Vader's help, the evil Empire wiped the Jedi out, and Obi-Wan was forced to go into hiding on Tatooine.

Nearly two decades later, Luke Skywalker brought Obi-Wan a message of hope. The Rebellion had a plan to defeat the Empire once and for all, and they needed Obi-Wan's help! Inspired by the potential he saw in Luke, Obi-Wan agreed to teach him the ways of the Force. But he dared not reveal the full truth—that Luke was actually Anakin Skywalker's son.

Obi-Wan journeyed with Luke and his friends to the Death Star, where he faced his old apprentice in battle one last time. Obi-Wan allowed Vader to defeat him so Luke Skywalker and his friends could get away. The Jedi Master became one with the Force after a lifetime of serving the galaxy for good.

ANAKIN SKYWALKER

Anakin was just a small slave boy on Tatooine the day the Jedi came and changed everything.

He and his mother, Shmi, were enslaved to the tricky junk dealer Watto. But Anakin was an excellent mechanic, and he could fly a podracer with lightning-fast precision.

Jedi Qui-Gon Jinn and Obi-Wan Kenobi needed young Anakin's help after landing on Tatooine in a ship that was in desperate need of repairs. The boy entered a podrace to win money for the parts the Jedi needed to fix their ship. Anakin won the race, and thanks to a bet Qui-Gon had made with Watto—the boy also won his own freedom!

Qui-Gon sensed that Anakin was strong in the

Force—so strong, in fact, that Qui-Gon believed Anakin was the prophesied Chosen One: the Jedi who would bring balance to the Force.

Qui-Gon, and later Obi-Wan, trained the boy. And Anakin was good! He could use the Force to overcome challenges and wield a lightsaber like no other Jedi before him. Perhaps he *was* the Chosen One.

But as Anakin's strength grew, so did his defiance. He became more arrogant to hide his deep-seated fear of losing the people he loved.

Along the way, Anakin met Padmé Amidala, a beautiful senator for the Republic and former queen of the planet Naboo. They shared a common background, having both assumed great power and responsibility at a young age. Anakin was charged with protecting Padmé during a trip to her home planet, and they quickly fell in love.

But Anakin's love for Padmé, and his fear of losing her, ultimately led to his downfall.

Darth Sidious, a Sith Lord disguised as the Galactic Senate's Chancellor Palpatine, wanted to use Anakin's powers for the dark side. He convinced Anakin that his power would be greater if he embraced his anger and hatred, luring the young man to the dark side of the Force.

After losing Padmé and fighting in a fateful battle against his former master, Obi-Wan Kenobi, the fallen Jedi was left broken and scarred.

Darth Sidious gave his new apprentice an imposing black robotic suit and mask, completing Anakin's transformation into the Sith Lord Darth Vader.

LUKE SKYWALKER

Luke Skywalker never knew his birth parents. His uncle Owen and aunt Beru raised him from a baby on the desert planet Tatooine. But as Luke grew into a young man, he couldn't shake the feeling that he was destined for something greater.

Luke's big chance came when his uncle purchased two droids from passing alien traders called Jawas. One droid, named C-3PO, was tall and gold and very anxious. The other droid, R2-D2, was short and silver and very loyal. Luke stumbled upon a hidden message from a Rebel Alliance leader named Princess Leia. The message, which R2 had recorded, was meant for Obi-Wan Kenobi. Luke and the droids found Obi-Wan across the desert.

To Luke's surprise, the older man revealed he was a Jedi!

Jedi Knights were powerful warriors who used the Force to defend peace and justice throughout the galaxy. They had all been defeated long before . . . or so everyone thought.

Obi-Wan said that Luke's father had also been a Jedi Knight, and he gave the boy his father's old lightsaber.

Obi-Wan began to teach Luke the ways of the Force while the two journeyed to deliver important information to the Rebellion. A smuggler named Han Solo and a Wookiee named Chewbacca joined them on their mission, and they soon found themselves entangled in intergalactic battles the likes of which Luke had never imagined he'd be a part of when he was back on Tatooine.

Using his impressive piloting skills and trusting his instincts through the Force, Luke helped the Rebel Alliance blow up the Empire's dreaded superweapon, the Death Star.

But his adventures weren't over yet. The Empire had a wide reach across the galaxy. Luke would need to face off against Darth Vader to save his friends and also discover his destiny. Darth Vader was, in fact, Luke Skywalker's father!

Vader had once been a masterful Jedi Knight named Anakin Skywalker. But the evil Sith Lord Darth Sidious—who was also the Emperor, who had taken control of the galaxy—had turned Anakin to the dark side of the Force.

The revelation shook Luke to his core. But Luke sensed that there was still good in his father—and he was right.

Luke Skywalker wasn't just a pilot, a rebel, and a Jedi—he was a hero!

THE EMPEROR

Darth Sidious lived his life fueled by the dark side of the Force. And he always had a plan: to take control of the galaxy.

Known to most as Emperor Palpatine, Sidious was a master manipulator, often giving orders from the shadows. His rise to power began when he was a senator for the Republic. Queen Amidala's home planet, Naboo, was invaded, and Palpatine offered counsel to the young queen on what to do. Little did Queen Amidala know, Palpatine had been behind the invasion himself! He convinced her to help him become chancellor of the Republic and then, later, Emperor. With total control, Palpatine took command of a clone army that would later become the first stormtrooper army of the Empire.

Even with so much influence, Sidious knew he required an apprentice. He first trained the fierce Sith Darth Maul. But after Obi-Wan Kenobi defeated Maul, Sidious, disguised as Palpatine, took an interest in Obi-Wan's own Padawan, Anakin Skywalker. He tricked the young Jedi into falling to the dark side. Together, they reorganized the Republic into the Galactic Empire—controlling the galaxy through tyranny and destroying any who stood in their way.

Darth Sidious's mastery of the dark side of the Force was so strong, he could shoot lightning out of his hands to electrocute his enemies. Despite all this, Luke Skywalker and the rebels were willing to stand up to his might. But the question remained: Was it even possible to defeat such a powerful foe?

DARTH MAUL

Darth Sidious's first apprentice, Darth Maul, was a fearsome Sith warrior who could slice and dice his way through any battle using his double-bladed lightsaber. He rarely spoke, but he didn't have to; he'd strike down his enemies before they even realized they were under attack.

The Jedi Order wasn't aware of Darth Maul's existence until the invasion of the planet Naboo. Maul was sent by Darth Sidious to capture Queen Amidala. But Jedi Masters Qui-Gon Jinn and Obi-Wan Kenobi thwarted his plot, forcing Darth Maul to reveal himself. The discovery caused grave concern for Yoda and the rest of the Jedi Council. There was no doubt this mysterious warrior was a Sith. "Always two there are," Yoda said, "a master and an apprentice."

Darth Maul returned to battle Qui-Gon and Obi-Wan while the inhabitants of Naboo fought for freedom. Wielding his fearsome double-bladed lightsaber, he clashed with the Jedi in the core generator room before defeating Qui-Gon. Obi-Wan was horrified, but he controlled his feelings just as Qui-Gon had taught him and used the Force to battle Darth Maul. With a well-timed strike, Obi-Wan defeated the evil Sith.

With Darth Maul gone, the Jedi Order had no way of determining who his evil master was. But it was only a matter of time before the phantom menace would be revealed.

COUNT DOOKU

Once a respected member of the Jedi Order, Count Dooku grew disgusted by the corruption he saw within the Republic. He thought the politicians were greedy, leaving poorer planetary systems to fend for themselves.

Whether Dooku was right or not to view the Republic as unjust, the steps he took next were truly evil. He sought power from the dark side to become Darth Tyranus and created the Confederacy of Independent Systems—a group of planets willing to rise up and destroy the Republic.

Obi-Wan Kenobi and Anakin Skywalker tried to stop Dooku, but the Sith Lord cornered them on the planet Geonosis. He gravely injured Obi-Wan with his blazing red lightsaber that had a curved hilt—and cut off Anakin's arm!

The Jedi were nearly done for when Yoda came to their rescue. Dooku and Yoda faced off in a ferocious lightsaber duel, and the small Grand Jedi Master revealed his true strength. Yoda flipped and whirled his green lightsaber so fast, Dooku couldn't fend off the attacks.

Desperate for a way to escape, Dooku caused a large pillar to fall on Obi-Wan and Anakin. Yoda was forced to use his concentration to save the Jedi, and Dooku took advantage of the distraction to flee.

But a few years later, Dooku was defeated once and for all by Anakin Skywalker.

DARTH VADER

Few names strike fear in the hearts of rebel fighters as much as Darth Vader. Just the sound of his deep, mechanical breathing means doom is around the corner.

Once a Jedi Knight named Anakin Skywalker, Vader was destroyed by searing lava during a battle with his former master, Obi-Wan Kenobi. The evil Emperor, Darth Sidious, revived Vader using a mechanical black suit of armor. But it came at a price: Vader became more machine than man. Twisted and evil, he helped destroy the Jedi and enforce the Empire's reign of terror across the galaxy.

When rebel leader Princess Leia tried to smuggle plans to the Rebel Alliance to help them defeat the Empire's superweapon, the Death Star, Vader stopped at

nothing to find her. Flanked by faithful stormtroopers, he attacked her ship and had the princess imprisoned. Vader easily fended off the rebels' blaster fire with his glowing red lightsaber, and he used the Force to choke his enemies without ever having to touch them.

Though Vader was evil through and through, when he learned that he had a son—Luke Skywalker—he wanted his son to join him in his quest for domination. He told Luke the truth about their connection during a battle on Cloud City. "Join me," he insisted, "and together, we will rule the galaxy as father and son."

Luke escaped from the battle gravely injured. But armed with the truth, he faced Vader again aboard the Empire's second Death Star and insisted Vader could be redeemed. The Emperor urged Luke to join the dark side or be destroyed. But in a shocking turn of events, Vader sacrificed himself to defeat the Emperor instead, saving Luke!

Before his death, the black-suited figure asked his son to remove his mask so Luke could see the scarred face of his father—Anakin Skywalker—and so Anakin could finally see his son with his own eyes.

STORMTROOPERS

Stormtroopers are the soldiers of the Empire. There are thousands of them, all wearing the same white armor and carrying blasters, ready to discipline any galactic citizen who opposes the Empire's will.

Stormtrooper armor is based on that of the original soldiers of the Galactic Republic, called clone troopers. Those soldiers fought alongside the Jedi in the Clone Wars and were actually clones, or copies, of a single bounty hunter named Jango Fett.

Once the Clone Wars concluded and Emperor Palpatine took control of the galaxy, he created the Galactic Empire and ordered legions of stormtroopers to be trained for supreme loyalty to the Empire.

There are different types of stormtroopers for different needs. For example, snowtroopers wear padded armor with face masks that protect them from the bitter cold on ice planets like Hoth. And scout troopers ride fast speeder bikes through rough terrain, like on the forest moon of Endor.

Deadly, persistent, and unwaveringly obedient, stormtroopers form the perfect fighting battalions to ensure the Empire's commands are carried out across the galaxy.

TIE FIGHTERS

Powered by twin ion engines, TIE fighters can zip through space wickedly fast and snipe rebel fighters in the blink of an eye. They're painted black and flown by pilots who trained at the Imperial Academy, making them both intimidating and deadly.

At the Battle of Yavin, the Empire's fleet of TIE fighters nearly stopped the rebels from blowing up the Death Star. Led by Darth Vader himself, the TIE fighters chased the X-wings straight into the battle station's trenches and zapped them before they could reach the thermal port leading to the reactor.

If Han Solo hadn't flown in at the last moment in the *Millennium Falcon* and blasted Darth Vader's Advanced TIE fighter away, Luke Skywalker would never have been able to blow up the Death Star.

TIE fighters come in lots of different models. For example, TIE bombers are able to drop relentless assaults of explosives on a planet. The Empire used them to try to scare Han Solo and Princess Leia out of hiding when they landed the *Millennium Falcon* in what they thought was an asteroid crater. Meanwhile, superfast TIE interceptors were the Empire's ship of choice during the Battle of Endor.

Whether for stealth, damage, or precision, TIE fighters are some of the Empire's strongest weapons.

STAR DESTROYERS

The main goal of the Empire is to exert control over the galaxy through fear. And the best way to do that is with really, *really* big battleships.

Imperial Star Destroyers are some of the most terrifying space cruisers in existence. These massive, wedge-shaped vessels are flying war machines, boasting turbolasers and tractor beams on nearly every surface. The underside is even a giant cargo bay that can open and release scores of TIE fighters at will.

If a Star Destroyer arrives in a planetary system, it means serious Imperial activity is afoot. Imagine how much trouble the rebels were in when they were piloting Princess Leia's tiny spacecraft toward Alderaan . . . and an Imperial Star Destroyer started chasing them!

Super Star Destroyers are even *larger* versions of normal Star Destroyers. They're so big, they can block an entire fleet of rebel ships simply by not moving. The Empire used this tactic during the space battle near Endor to prevent the rebels from escaping. The Super Star Destroyer loomed in space, not allowing any rebel ships to pass, while the Empire's second Death Star picked them off one by one. Talk about a losing battle!

THE
REBELLION

PRINCESS LEIA

Princess Leia is a born leader, cool under pressure yet always ready to jump headfirst into a fight to defend her friends. She hails from the planet Alderaan, and while she may seem like a reserved diplomat, Leia is really a leader in the Rebel Alliance working to covertly overthrow the evil Empire and restore freedom to the galaxy!

Leia's most daring mission came when she received top-secret plans from other rebel fighters. The schematics revealed a weakness in the Empire's dreaded superweapon, the Death Star. It was up to Princess Leia to deliver the plans to the Rebel Alliance base, but before she could, her ship was captured by Darth Vader and his fleet!

Thinking fast, Leia hid the plans in a droid named

R2-D2 and directed the little astromech to use an escape shuttle to take the information to Jedi Master Obi-Wan Kenobi on the planet Tatooine. Darth Vader soon boarded her ship, wiping out her guards and taking the princess prisoner. Even still, Leia wouldn't be intimidated. She refused to tell Vader where the plans were, willing to risk her own life for the Rebellion.

With Luke Skywalker and Han Solo's aid, Leia escaped from the Death Star and later helped lead the battle to blow it up. Her determination is second only to her ability to strategize. As a rebel leader, Leia organized the rebels' evacuation during the attack on Echo Base on the ice planet Hoth. And she even drove a speeder bike through the thick forest of Endor's moon to outsmart stormtroopers during the final conflict with the Empire.

Along the way, Leia faced many enemies who underestimated her bravery. She went undercover as a bounty hunter to rescue Han Solo when he was held frozen in carbonite by the crime boss Jabba the Hutt. And when she was enslaved, she waited for just the right moment to attack the vile sluglike Hutt and win back her freedom. Regal and courageous, Princess Leia knows it is only through perseverance and trust in her friends that the galaxy can be freed once more.

C-3PO & R2-D2

The galaxy is filled with droids of all shapes and sizes, but few are as loyal to the Rebellion as R2-D2 and C-3PO.

Their story goes back almost all the way to the beginning of the conflict, well before the Empire rose to power.

R2-D2 is a droid who speaks in a language of beeps and boops. Originally, he served as an astromech for the defense fleet of Naboo. Astromechs are droids that help pilots control their ships, plotting courses, firing weapons, and even making crucial repairs during battle.

R2-D2 helped a very young Anakin Skywalker control a starfighter during the fight for Naboo's freedom, and decades later, he helped Anakin's son,

Luke Skywalker, do the same during the battle against the Death Star.

Meanwhile, C-3PO's history runs even deeper. He was actually *built* by young Anakin Skywalker. Anakin designed the protocol droid to help his mom when they were slaves on Tatooine. But as time went on, C-3PO proved his talent for human-cyborg relations, becoming fluent in over six million forms of communication. At times he's bumbling, but his intentions are always good.

R2-D2 and C-3PO met on Tatooine and became best friends. They traveled the universe together, going on many daring missions. C-3PO worries about everything, while R2-D2 stays calm under pressure, making these two perfect companions.

C-3PO would never admit he and the little droid are best buddies, though. He often quips that R2-D2 is a "bucket of bolts" or an "overweight glob of grease," while R2-D2 fires back zingers in his beeps and boops that C-3PO is usually too offended by to translate. But these droids have been there for each other during even the direst situations. In a galaxy of uncertainty, they can always count on each other.

X-WINGS

X-wings are the rebels' go-to battle aircraft.

Named for their cross-winged shape, these deft ships are armed with four laser cannons and two proton torpedo launchers. They can even make the jump to lightspeed, so they can sneak up on enemy fighters out of the blue!

Each X-wing is piloted by a rebel fighter and an astromech droid. When things are looking bleak, a pilot can always trust his or her astromech to come through in a pinch.

These clever little droids are able to fix a broken laser cannon, launch weapons, and even take over flying the ship if the pilot is injured.

During battle, the rebels divide their X-wings into

groups called squadrons. Each fighter goes by a call sign. Luke Skywalker's call sign is Red Five, and his good friend Wedge Antilles is Red Two.

The rebels used X-wings to take on not one but *two* Death Stars!

It just goes to show that even the mightiest weapons of the Empire could be defeated by the tiniest rebel fighters as long as the rebels had courage.

THE MILLENNIUM FALCON

HAN SOLO

Bold, brazen, and filled with enough swagger to charm even a Wookiee, Han Solo is one of the galaxy's best smugglers. He's the pilot of the *Millennium Falcon*, "the fastest ship in the galaxy." With a blaster on his hip and his best friend and copilot, Chewbacca the Wookiee, at his side, Han Solo is ready to take on anything.

Han's greatest adventure began when a wise old man and a wide-eyed kid tracked him down at Mos Eisley spaceport on Tatooine—the most wretched hive of scum and villainy in that quadrant. The old man and boy were none other than Obi-Wan Kenobi and Luke Skywalker. They needed a ship—a fast ship. "My ship's fast enough for you, old man," Han promised. "But it'll cost you."

During their mission to rescue the princess and

escape the Death Star, Han proved his prowess when he and Chewie fought back a legion of stormtroopers on their own. Instead of just firepower, Han used the power of deception to convince the stormtroopers he was wild—by running straight at them! The stormtroopers were completely confused, giving Han's friends Luke and Leia enough time to make it back to the *Millennium Falcon* safely.

But perhaps Han's greatest claim to fame is his skill as a pilot. He can jump the *Falcon* to lightspeed faster than blaster fire, and he's just as quick with a laser cannon.

After years of smuggling and flying under the Empire's radar, Han learned to watch out for himself and trust no one, other than Chewbacca. The only reason he agreed to help Obi-Wan and Luke rescue Leia in the first place was because he knew he'd be paid well for the job. But he never expected to find the true friends he met in the Rebellion. When it mattered the most, Han came through for them. In the battle against the Death Star, he flew on the scene just in time to save Luke from Darth Vader's Advanced TIE fighter, allowing Luke to fire the victory shot that blew up the massive superweapon. It turned out this rogue smuggler wasn't just interested in money. He had a heart of gold, as well.

CHEWBACCA

It's not easy for a tall, furry Wookiee to blend in, but Chewbacca doesn't need to. He's one of the most confident fighters in the galaxy, and he uses his size to his advantage. After all, an enemy will think twice before making a Wookiee angry!

Chewbacca (also known as Chewie) is the copilot of the *Millennium Falcon* and Han Solo's best friend. The two met when they were both captured by Imperial forces and Han helped Chewie escape. (Though if Chewie was telling the story, he might say it was the other way around!) Chewie speaks in roars and growls that can be frightening at first. But usually he's just complaining about something, like losing at holochess or how bad a place smells.

Chewie's weapon of choice is an energy bowcaster.

His fighting skills came in handy when the rebels were battling the Empire on the forest moon of Endor. Chewbacca managed to take control of an AT-ST walker, a powerful robot that walked through the forest and shot anything in its path. At the controls, Chewie used the AT-ST to take out other Imperial AT-STs and turn the tide of the battle. He even made some new furry friends along the way: the small bearlike inhabitants of Endor, called Ewoks.

From smuggler to copilot to rebel warrior, Chewbacca is someone any fighter would be proud to call a friend.

THE FASTEST SHIP
IN THE GALAXY

The *Millennium Falcon* is Han Solo's pride and joy. He won it in a card game against Lando Calrissian, another infamous smuggler. And Han will eagerly boast to anyone who will listen that the *Millennium Falcon* made the Kessel Run in twelve parsecs (which is extremely fast).

Though it may look like a hunk of junk, this ship has outrun Imperial starships, outmaneuvered fleets of TIE fighters, and even escaped the jaws of a ginormous space slug!

Han and Leia were running out of options during a particularly desperate attempt to get away from the Empire when they careened directly into an asteroid field. Thinking fast, Han flew the ship inside an asteroid crater to hide from the Empire. Little did

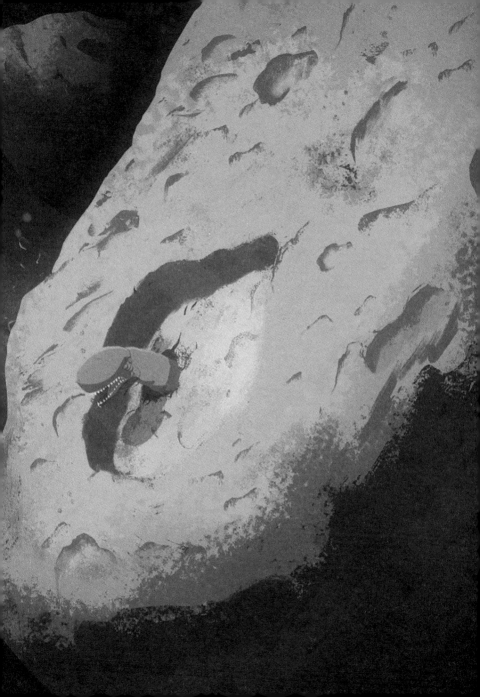

they know, the cave they'd flown into was actually the mouth of a massive space slug. Han steered the ship out of the creature's jaws just in time. But it was a close call!

The *Falcon* also came to the rescue of the rebels during the Battle of Endor. Han reluctantly allowed Lando Calrissian to fly the *Falcon* into battle against the Death Star. Lando promised he'd return the ship in one piece, with a victory to boot.

It may not be the prettiest starship in the galaxy, but it definitely has a few tricks left up its sleeve.

SCUM & VILLAINY

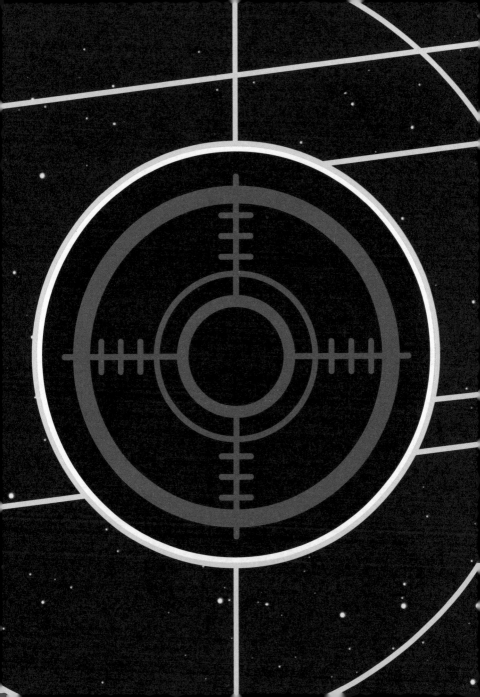

JABBA THE HUTT

Jabba the Hutt is the most powerful crime boss on the desert planet Tatooine. He belongs to a species of aliens called Hutts, known for their sluglike appearance and massive appetites. His palace on Tatooine is a den of greed and gluttony.

Jabba's criminal specialty is smuggling illegal goods while avoiding the watchful eye of the Empire. He employs rogues of all kinds to do his dirty work—and bounty hunters to track down any who dare double-cross him.

For years, Han Solo worked as a smuggler for Jabba. Business was good, since Han had a fast ship and could charm his way out of pretty much anything. But when Han got boarded by Imperial troops during a smuggling run and had to dump his cargo, Jabba was furious. He put a price so high on Han's head, every bounty hunter in the galaxy was out looking for him!

Eventually, Han was captured by the deadly bounty hunter Boba Fett, frozen in carbonite, and turned over to the sluglike crime boss. Jabba put the block of carbonite on display in his palace like a statue! Han was alive inside, yet trapped.

Princess Leia came to Han's rescue disguised as a bounty hunter, but Jabba discovered her plan and had her enslaved.

It was only during a daring rescue mission by Luke Skywalker that the tables finally turned. Han was freed, and Leia managed to defeat the disgusting crime boss using the very chain he'd imprisoned her with.

Jabba the Hutt may have enjoyed the greatest criminal fortune on Tatooine, but his luck had finally run out.

BOBA FETT

Boba Fett is the most feared bounty hunter in the galaxy. He's been on countless missions to track down fugitives with prices on their heads. And his missions all have one thing in common: he's never failed.

Known for his weathered green Mandalorian armor and silent manner, Boba Fett learned the ways of bounty hunting from his father, Jango Fett. As a boy, Boba lived with Jango on the planet Kamino. The aliens there paid Jango to be a "template" from which they would clone troopers for the Grand Army of the Republic. In addition to his sizable pay, Jango asked the Kamino aliens for one thing: an unaltered clone he could raise as his son. That clone was Boba.

Jango taught Boba everything he knew about bounty hunting, from deadly combat techniques to flying skills. But when Jango was killed by Jedi Master Mace Windu, Boba Fett swore vengeance on the Jedi.

Darth Vader gave Boba Fett his highest-profile mission of all when he ordered him to track down Han Solo. Vader wanted to use Han as bait to trap Luke Skywalker, and in return, the Sith Lord agreed that Boba could take Han to Jabba the Hutt and collect the bounty on Han's head.

Boba trailed Han to the floating Cloud City above Bespin. He and Darth Vader tricked Lando Calrissian, the administrator of Cloud City and Han's friend, into helping them capture Han . . . and freeze him in carbonite!

Boba delivered Han to Jabba. But he had underestimated the lengths Han's friends would go to in order to rescue their trapped companion.

In a final climactic battle for Han's freedom, Boba Fett faced off against Luke Skywalker over the Great Pit of Carkoon on Tatooine. It was a showdown that would determine Han's fate, as well as the bounty hunter's.

GALACTIC BATTLES

BATTLE OF YAVIN

Outpowered, outnumbered, and outgunned, the rebels had only one thing going for them as they entered the Battle of Yavin: hope.

They knew they needed to defeat the Empire's massive planet-killing machine, the Death Star. But with their small ships and even smaller numbers, it seemed like an impossible task. Fortunately, Princess Leia had smuggled plans that revealed a single weakness in the battle station. There was a small thermal exhaust port leading from the outside of the Death Star straight to the main reactor. If the rebels could fire a single shot into that port, the blast would hit the main reactor, causing a chain reaction that would blow up the Death Star.

Luke Skywalker insisted it could be done. Together

with a squadron of X-wings, he flew into battle against the Death Star.

TIE fighters zoomed straight at them. Laser shots from the enemy ships whizzed this way and that. The rebels rolled their starships through space to avoid the blasts. But one by one they were taken out, and their small numbers were dwindling. When Luke finally made it into the trench running along the Death Star, he was all by himself, and he had just one shot.

Then Darth Vader chased Luke in his Advanced TIE fighter, locking his torpedo targets on Luke. But at the last moment, Han Solo flew in with the *Millennium Falcon* and blasted Darth Vader's TIE fighter away! Vader's ship went spiraling into space. "You're all clear, kid!" Han shouted over the radio. "Now let's blow this thing and go home!"

Trusting his instincts in the Force, Luke fired his ship's proton torpedoes. It was a direct hit! The Death Star blew up in a fiery explosion. The Rebel Alliance was ecstatic. Darth Vader had survived, but the rebels had dealt a massive blow to the Empire.

BATTLE OF HOTH

Infuriated by their defeat at the Battle of Yavin, the Empire sought a way to strike back at the Rebel Alliance. They found that opportunity in the icy Battle of Hoth.

The Empire sent out hundreds of probe droids to scour the galaxy, and one droid found the rebels' secret Echo Base on the snow-covered planet. The Empire launched a full-force attack with AT-AT walkers on the surface while a Star Destroyer blocked escape in space.

Thinking fast, the rebels used ion cannons to fire at the Star Destroyer while their transport ships hurried to evacuate the rebel troops from the base.

Meanwhile, Luke Skywalker led a snowspeeder defense against the AT-ATs. But the AT-ATs were so big

and powerful, the snowspeeders weren't able to blow them up with blaster fire.

"We have to use our tow cables," Luke said. "It may be our only chance."

Luke instructed the other pilots to attach their tow cables to the legs of the AT-AT walkers and fly around the machines in circles, literally tying them up.

His plan worked: the AT-ATs tripped and toppled!

But despite the rebels' efforts, the Empire's forces were too strong. They reached the main generator for Echo Base and blew it up.

What was left of the rebel forces retreated. The Empire had taken the upper hand.

BATTLE OF ENDOR

At the Battle of Endor, the Rebel Alliance would either defeat the evil that had controlled the galaxy for so long or be destroyed by it.

It had been four years since the destruction of the Death Star at the Battle of Yavin. In that time, Luke Skywalker had trained to become a full Jedi Master, and the rebels had regrouped their forces after the destruction of Echo Base on Hoth. But the Empire had also been busy: it had built a new, even more powerful Death Star. And soon it would be ready to start blowing up planets!

With the help of Bothan spies, the rebels learned that the Death Star was in the final stages of completion over the forest moon of Endor. And the Emperor himself was on board overseeing the work!

This was the rebels' one and only shot to defeat the Empire for good.

They sent a rebel team led by Han, Luke, and Leia to the moon's surface. Their mission was to deactivate the force field generator so the rebel ships could attack the Death Star. But reaching the generator wouldn't be easy. Not only was it guarded by scout troopers, but the rebels caught the attention of the fuzzy little Ewoks who lived on the planet, too.

The Ewoks thought the rebels were enemies, but C-3PO convinced the creatures that the rebels were their friends. In fact, they made such an impression, the Ewoks agreed to help the rebels in their fight.

Meanwhile, up in space, Admiral Ackbar and Lando Calrissian led the aerial attack on the Death Star. But they were in for a nasty surprise. The Emperor and Darth Vader knew they were coming, and the Death Star was fully operational!

The Sith Lord's real plan all along had been to trick the rebels into attacking so he could capture Luke Skywalker and turn the young Jedi to the dark side by threatening the destruction of his friends.

Together, Vader and the Emperor lured Luke aboard the Death Star and forced him into a lightsaber duel that would determine his destiny.

From the battle on the forest moon to the starship fight in space to the lightsaber duel between father and son on the Death Star, the Battle of Endor was the climactic conclusion to the Galactic Civil War.

Against all odds, the rebels managed to defeat the Empire, destroying the second Death Star, freeing the galaxy, and proving that the Force really was with them.